DR. CYNDI MADISON-ARNOLD

Satan You Have Just Been Hacked
drcyndispeakslife@gmail.com

All scriptures are from the King James Version of the bible unless otherwise noted.

Entegrity Choice Publishing
PO Box 453
Powder Springs, GA 30127
info@entegritypublishing.com
www.entegritypublishing.com
404.472.9190

Printed in the United States of America

Library of Congress Cataloging-in-Publication Data
ISBN 979-8-9991668-0-7
Library of Congress Control Number: 2025912394

DEDICATION

I dedicate this book to my parents, the late Fred L. Williams, Sr. and the late Annie M. Williams as well as all of my spiritual parents who influenced my life through the years: the late Bishop Jonathan Greer II; Prophetess Juanita Bynum; Bishop Paul S. Morton; Bishop Arthur F. Mosley; my mother in love, Mrs. Omie Jean Haynes, who showed me so much love after the loss of my mother; and my amazing husband, Charles A. Arnold, for loving me, honoring the Woman of God within me, and your dedication and patience while I was writing this book. I love you to life, sweetheart.

CONTENTS

FOREWORD

IN THIS SEASON OF CHAOS AND FEAR, the Holy Spirit has led Dr. Cyndi Madison-Arnold to teach and enlighten all who read and receive this book and to empower them to handle anything that comes their way!

Satan, You Have Just Been Hacked is a much-needed gift in the Body of Christ. Get ready to be empowered with spiritual strategies, spiritual insight, and faith-driven action steps you need to hack into Satan and the kingdom of darkness to disrupt his plans. Through the power of the Holy Spirit, I decree and declare that you will *intercept, cancel,* and *make void* every satanic plot and plan of the enemy against you, your family, your church, your community, your state, and your nation.

". . . but the people that do know their God shall be strong, and do exploits."
—Daniel 11:32 (KJV)

I have been blessed over the years to have a front-row seat to witness how Dr. Madison-Arnold walks in the deep things of God. She is anointed, powerful, equipped, and knowledgeable to teach and minister the spiritual blueprint on how you can know God and do exploits for the Kingdom of God.

In *Satan, You Have Just Been Hacked,* Dr. Madison-Arnold drives a stake into the heart of the kingdom of darkness. After reading this powerful book, it is my prayer that you will walk in purpose and power, demonstrating to a lost and dark world the POWER of God in action! I encourage you to be strong in the Lord and in the power of His might!

Read these pages carefully and in anticipation because you will never live the same again!

Pastor Roxie Hairston
Reaching Beyond the Break Ministries
Founder, Entegrity Choice Publishing
Atlanta, Georgia

INTRODUCTION

"He reveals deep and secret things; He knows what lies in darkness, and light dwells with Him."
—Daniel 2:22

God Only Reveals His Secrets to Believers

There is spiritual warfare going on in the world today, and God has anointed me to impart something in your spirit to help you deal with Satan and his cohorts of darkness that cannot be reversed. Satan's greatest desire is to be ignored; he wants us to look at the outside of a person, at their race or ethnicity, rather than look inside where the spirit dwells and operates daily within all of humanity. The Word of God declares that there are vessels of honor and vessels of dishonor among us.

In 2 Timothy 2:20–21, Paul uses this vessel metaphor to describe how God chooses some people as human vessels for His use, while Satan chooses other people as human vessels for his use here on Earth. The more you submit to God's commandments, the more He can use your vessel to represent Him here on Earth.

The more you choose to submit to Satan's ways, the more you are preparing your human vessel to be accessed by the supernatural spirit of darkness where Satan himself dwells here on Earth. You see, Satan doesn't have a human body, and the only way he can do his evil on Earth is through a physical human body.

God has inspired me to write this novella to share with the Body of Christ. Jesus came from Heaven to Earth to show us how to live our best Christian life here on Earth. God has given me a series of short stories to encourage some and give hope to others in the Body of Christ.

"In all of your ways acknowledge Him and
He will make straight your path."
—Proverbs 3:6 NIV

In my 40 years being a saved, sanctified, blood-washed, born-again believer walking with Christ, I have learned how to trust God for every one of my needs and how to be content with whatever I have.

Satan Is the Father of Lies

Satan has been deceiving humanity since the beginning in the Garden of Eden, and so I have written this book to empower you to turn the tables on him and his cohorts of darkness here on Earth. Revelation 12:4 tells us God evicted Satan from Heaven when he rebelled against God, and he took one-third of the angels with him. This book will equip you with biblical knowledge, spiritual strategies, and faith-driven action steps to dismantle his schemes and walk FREELY IN THE LIGHT from him and his evil devices here on Earth. God Himself came all the way from Heaven to Earth wrapped up in a man called Jesus to give you victory! The Word of God declares, *"Submit your ways to God. Resist the devil, and he will flee from you."* (James 4:7 NKJV)

Get ready! Get ready! Get ready! Buckle up because this book is about take you on a journey into the deep secrets things of God and the deep spiritual warfare we encounter each day from Satan and his cohorts of darkness here with us on Earth. Are you ready to hack into Satan's lies and deception and reclaim the spiritual authority given to every blood-washed, born-again believer when our Lord and Savior Jesus Christ got up from the cross? Let's get it!

We Walk By Faith and Not By Sight

I have learned how to live on almost nothing or with everything. I have learned the secret of living in every situation, whether it is with a full or empty stomach, with plenty or little. For I can do everything through Christ who gives me strength. Rather I was single, divorced, or married during these turbulent and trying times in my life God revealed to me that He was pruning me to produce more fruit.

> *"Who shall separate us from the love of Christ, tribulation or distress or persecution or famine or nakedness or peril or sword? For I am convinced that neither death nor life, neither angels nor demons, neither the present nor the future, nor any powers, neither height nor depth, nor anything else in all creation, shall separate us from His love."*
>
> —Romans 8:35–39

We saints, born-again believers, church folks, single, divorced, and married alike must learn how to trust God regardless of our circumstances because we will face trials and tribulations daily. We must never give up on God. The Holy Spirit has given us a relentless faith, a resiliency in God that the world cannot comprehend, a peace that surpasses all understanding, and a renewed mind that transforms us daily to be ready for the fight of our lives.

2 Corinthians 5:7 declares, *"We walk by faith and not by sight."* Therefore, we must activate our faith daily to be overcomers by using our power for living, which comes directly from the Word of God and the Holy Spirit. My book's title, *Satan, You Have Just Been Hacked*, is a testament to God's faithfulness to believers, to how He reveals Himself to us in the thick of our darkness, and to how He reveals to us those things to come that are in darkness to the world. He gives light to His true believers. In John 15:1–17, Jesus referred to Himself as the true vine, us as the branches, and God as the vine dresser. We must pray and study the Word of God daily to stay connected to the true vine (Jesus). The Word of God declares that God will speak to you in multiple ways to guide you on your Christian journey.

How To Be Sure You Are Hearing God's Voice?

There are multiple ways that God will speak to you if you are in relationship and fellowship with him daily. He will speak to you through prayer and meditation.

God's voice communicates with your spirit, not your five senses or your flesh. To hear God's voice you must understand that He is a Holy Spirit, and those who worship Him must worship Him in spirit and in truth (John 4:24). Therefore, you must pray, fast, and meditate on the Word of God to position your spirit to hear God's voice.

"He who has ears to hear, let him hear."
—Mark 4:9

My prayer is that this anointed, God-inspired novella will empower you and that God will give you an ear to hear when He is speaking directly to your heart for you to follow the plans that He has already ordained for your life before the foundation of this world. He will also speak to you through prophets, friends, family members, pastors, teachers, and children.

"For I know the plans I have for you, plans to prosper you and not to harm you, plans to give you hope and a future."
—Jeremiah 29:11

"God has raised believers up with Christ and seated us in heavenly places in Christ Jesus while we were still sinners."
—Ephesians 2:6

We must take God at His word that we have power that the world cannot see or understand. We must live a lifestyle of holiness to be the light of the world as Christ ordained us to be in Matthew 5:14 NLT: *"You are the Light of the world . . . like a city on a hilltop that cannot be hidden."*

PART

I

Satan is the God of This World

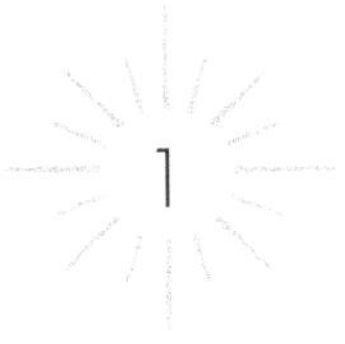

God Has Given Us His Dominus Power to Overcome Every Attack of Satan

WE KNOW THAT SATAN IS OUR ADVERSARY and not our friend; his desire is to sift us as wheat. Satan hates God and is his chief adversary. Every time Satan attacks a born-again believer, he is not attacking us, but the God in us.

I remember the time when I met someone who appeared to be a lifetime partner; however, my God-given spirit of discernment kicked in, and I began to feel unsure about this person's character, even though they were being extremely generous to show me love. God then brought this person to me in a dream or vision and showed me him fighting against him in the pulpit; he was looking up to Heaven at the time of this fight, and he eventually destroyed the whole podium in the pulpit in my dream. I learned many years later that this dream revelation was God showing me that this person spirit wasn't necessarily fighting against God in Heaven; rather, he was fighting against the spirit of God that was within me.

Satan dwells in the extraterrestrial so he can see and operate in the spirit realm of darkness where he dwells. The saints who are born again and filled with the Holy Spirit should be able to recognize Satan by using their discernment of spirits. When we meet someone new in our lives, they represent one spirit—either the spirit of God or the spirit of Satan. Each day we wake up and begin our day, Satan hates when we put our feet on the floor because he knows that we are on God's assignment and that God has indoctrinated us into His kingdom.

We are God's chosen vessels to represent Him and His work here on Earth. Jesus came to destroy Satan's works here on Earth. Satan knows who you are in the spirit realm, and his assignment and desire for your life is to sift you as wheat. Jesus instructed his disciples to "watch and pray, that ye enter not into temptation; the spirit indeed is willing, but the flesh is weak." Satan knows our weaknesses and will always appear as an angel of light. We always want to assume that the people we meet every day are good and not evil. It's only when we get to know them later on that we began to see their true nature; we know that the fruit does not fall too far from the tree.

For saints to hack into Satan's dark works in the world, you must be born again. In conversation with Nicodemus, Jesus said, *"Most assuredly, I say to you, unless one is born of water and the Spirit, he cannot enter the kingdom of God. That which is born of the flesh is flesh, and that which is born of the Spirit is spirit. Do not marvel that I said to you, 'You must be born again.' The wind blows where it wishes, and you hear it, but cannot tell where it comes from and where it goes. So is everyone who is born of the Spirit."* (John 3:5–8 NKJV)

Satan dwells in his kingdom of darkness. He has an army of followers here on Earth who are part of his kingdom of darkness and can be on multiple assignments simultaneously. What exactly are Satan's works? There are several passages in the Word of God; Jesus gives us a clear and precise look at Satan's work in John 8:44. Confronting the hypocritical religious leaders of Israel, Jesus said, *"You belong to your father, the devil, and you want to carry out your father's desires. He was a murderer from the beginning, not holding to truth, for there is no truth in him. When Satan lies, he speaks his native language, for he is a liar and the father of lies."*

According to Jesus, some of Satan's works are murder and lying. These two sins summarize Satan's character and goals. He works to see people destroyed and to go hell (that's murder), and he desires to deceive them into that destruction (that's lying).

Satan's work showed up in the Garden of Eden, where he deceived Eve and led her into disobedience (Genesis 3:1–6). As a result, Adam also sinned and threw humanity into the bondage of sin (Romans 5:12). Satan lied to Eve with the goal of murdering her (that is, separating her from God); he wanted humanity to die (spiritually).

Before we were saved, we were under the full effects of Satan's works. In fact, we "were in our transgressions and sins, in which we used to live when we followed the ways of this world and the ruler of the kingdom of the air, the Spirit who is now at work in those who are disobedient." (Ephesians 2:1–2)

We can see Satan operating in our nation today at the highest level of politics. We have a leader in a position of great power, and one of Satan's greatest desires is for our leader to bring harm and evil, even death, on the less fortunate and marginalized communities. Satan has zero compassion for humanity.

Satan's work in our lives have caused some of us to be "gratifying the cravings of our flesh and following its desires and thoughts."

It is only through the love, mercy, and grace of God that we have been rescued from the works of Satan. The works of Satan affect humanity morally, physically, intellectually, and most of all, spiritually. Morally, Satan entices the weak and the feeble who do not know God into sin, making evil seem appealing so that people choose evil over obedience to God (James 1:14).

Physically, Satan can inflict disease, and he seeks to use physical trials to cause people to curse God. Intellectually, Satan seduces those who are in darkness into error, teaching false doctrines. For example, 1 Timothy 4:1 tells us that Satan casts doubt and keeps unbelievers intellectually blinded to spiritual truth and the gospel, while 2 Corinthians 4:3–4 tells us that Satan arranges distractions and promotes confusion that cause people to act hastily, irrationally, and foolishly. Spiritually, Satan takes every opportunity to snatch away the word of God sown into a person's heart.

> *"When anyone hears the word of the kingdom*
> *and does not understand it, then Satan comes and*
> *snatches it away what was sown in his heart."*
> —Matthew 13:19

This passage represents the parable of the seed in the Word of God, the seed that is sown in the person's heart. If the person doesn't understand the Word, Satan snatches away the seed. The seed that fell on the path represents people who hear the message but don't understand it, and the birds that eat the seed represent Satan. The "word of the kingdom" refers to the Gospel, which describes the person, office, and grace of the king Messiah. It also describes the kingdom of grace that saints enjoy now, and the kingdom of Heaven they will enter in the future.

The devil's desire is to attack believers. Satan will try to cause believers not to follow Christ so as to keep them from their primary assignment and purpose here on Earth, which is to bring God glory and further His purposes and plans for their lives. If Satan can entice us into addictions such as drugs, alcohol, entertainment, sex, and porn, then he sets traps for us to bring us into his bondage so that we cannot commune with God, because sin separates us from God. We will then lose our testimony before family, friends, and the world.

In summary, as saints we must acknowledge that Satan's works of darkness are counter to God's works of light here on Earth.

- As a murderer, Satan works against God, who gives us life and light.
- As a liar, Satan works against God, who is truth.
- In the lives of believers and unbelievers, Satan's goal is to keep you from accepting Christ.
- In the lives of believers and unbelievers, Satan's goal is to tempt you into sin.
- In the lives of unbelievers, Satan's goal is to block you from Heaven.
- In the lives of unbelievers, Satan's goal is to keep you from eternal life

Fortunately for us, Jesus Christ came all the way from Heaven to Earth to destroy Satan's works. As his arrest and crucifixion drew near, Jesus said, *"Now is the judgment on this world, now the prince of this world will be driven out."* (John 12:31)

Jesus accomplished many amazing things on the cross. He took the penalty for our sins and gave us His righteousness. Therefore, the devil has no power over our eternal destiny as believers in Christ.

It isn't that Satan can't or won't tempt us as saints to sin. He may occasionally succeed. It's that Jesus's death bore all the wrath of God against sin, and God doesn't see or hold our sins against us as long as we repent (Romans 8:1).

God sees the blood that was shed on the cross. Not only did Jesus's death destroy Satan's works in relation to our eternal destiny, but it provided for our personal sanctification. Believers have the gift of the Holy Spirit who dwells in us and leads us into being transformed in the likeness of our Lord and Savior Jesus Christ. The Holy Spirit has sealed us to believe in Christ, and Satan cannot remove us from our promises (Ephesians 4:30).

By God's goodness and mercy, the Lord has also given us spiritual dominus power, which is a mighty weapon to do battle with Satan. Satan might bring a lot of things on us, but if we keep ourselves suited up in God's armor, the battle will be much easier. We must understand our enemy and recognize when he is approaching: *"We are not unaware of Satan's schemes of darkness and to see our demise."* (2 Corinthians 2:11)

We must understand our enemy and know where our strength and defense are and trust God during these times on Earth and in our lives like never before. Jesus the perfecter of our faith (Hebrews 12:2), the only one who can truly destroy Satan's works.

We serve a God who is a sovereign God

- God is supreme and has no equal in authority or power,
- God has the power, wisdom, and authority to do anything he chooses,
- God is responsible for the creation of everything,
- God is outside of time and has no beginning or end, and
- God holds all creation together.

How does God's sovereignty relate to human free will?

- God has given humans the freedom to choose.
- God has a plan for humans.
- Humans will give an account to God for their choices and behaviors.
- Gods' sovereignty is related to the concept of human free will.

Examples of God's sovereignty

- God's control over the nations
- God's control over the weather
- God's control over all the details of life
- God's control souls in heaven and in hell

The Word of God teaches us about God's sovereignty and why it is absolute and includes control over all things. Additional works of his sovereignty are the following:

- **Creation:** God created the universe, including our bodies, personalities, and souls.

- **Weather:** God controls the weather and its effects.
- **Life:** God controls all the details of life, including seemingly random events such as rolling dice.
- **People:** God controls nations and people's souls.
- **Jonah's mission:** God prepared the fish, plant, and worm to ensure Jonah's mission was not left to chance.
- **Jesus's death:** God was in control of every detail of Jesus's death, including the fulfillment of prophecy.
- **Suffering:** God allows suffering to work together for good.

Indeed, we only really find comfort in God's sovereignty when we learn to trust Him. If we fearfully dread that one day He will break his word, or turn evil, or relinquish power, we will not have peace. Or, if we demand to know why God's sovereignty acts as it does, we will grow bitter and angry.

God is the supernatural, omnipresent being, which means He is always everywhere. In this world filled with daily challenges, spiritual battles, and uncertainties, many believers struggle to walk in the fullness of God's authority. However, the Word of God makes it clear that as children of God, we are not powerless, and we have dominion and power that the world cannot see. God has given us spiritual authority, and once we recognize our divine identity that sets us apart from this world, Satan and his cohorts of darkness will no longer deceive us.

Satan gets his power from lies and deception, leading many nonbelievers and believers alike to see themselves as weak, unworthy, unloved, and powerless in their minds when they focus on their circumstances and not on the Word of God. But as you traverse

Satan, You Have Just Been Hacked, you will gain access to a deeper wisdom, knowledge, and understanding of God's power within you, your promise of a heavenly citizenship with streets paved with gold, and your identity in Christ as a blood-washed, born-again believer.

You were created to worship your creator and not the creature here on Earth. You were created to walk in dominion and resist Satan's world of darkness and influence here on Earth. You were created to live in holy boldness as a conqueror and a winner, not a loser. You were born to win. The fight is fixed if you confessed with your mouth and believe in your heart that Jesus Christ is your Lord and Savior in your life. Be encouraged and let Satan know that you will no longer walk in darkness and be tossed to and fro by the waves and carried about by the wind of doctrine, by human cunning, by craftiness in deceitful schemes.

The God you serve has hacked all of Satan's deceptive and evil devices with his infinite powers. The God you serve is Alpha and Omega. He knows the end of your situation at the beginning. Therefore, when Satan attacks, you will win!

This is your season to step into your God-given authority. God has ordered your steps today to embark on this transformative journey using the Word of God as your weapon of warfare, standing firm on your faith and walking in total victory every time Satan and his cohorts of darkness attack you and your family, be it your health, your finances, your family, your jobs, your business, your church family, your children, and even your grandchildren! We have the VICTORY if we apply the Word of God, which is the "Light of the World" to every area of your daily lives.

Satan's final destination is hell. The lake of fire was designated for Satan and his fallen angels (Matthew 25:41). That will be their ultimate destiny. Our sovereign God has decided not to provide salvation to fallen angelic beings (Hebrews 2:16).

We Are in the World But Not of the World

THE WORD OF GOD DECLARES that we believers should be in the world but not of the world. Meaning that we should live in the world but not share its values and beliefs.

Instead, we as born-again believers should follow the teachings of our Lord and Savior Jesus Christ. Paul said, *"Let this mind be in you that was also in Christ Jesus."* (Philippians 2:5)

In John 17:15–16, Jesus says, *"I have given them your word, and the world has hated them because they are not of the world, even as I am not of the world. I do not ask you to take them out of the world, but to keep them from the evil one (Satan). They are not of the world even as I am not of the world."*

Believers are called to be holy and set apart. Believers should be holy and righteous and not participate in the world and Satan's sinful activities designed for those who walk in darkness.

Believers should be ambassadors for Christ.

Believers are called to live in the world as ambassadors for our Lord and Savior Jesus Christ, as though God were making an appeal through us; we beg you on the behalf of Christ to be reconciled to God.

Believers are called to a daily commitment to live a life that reflects Christ's word and values and not to conform to the world's trends.

Believers are commanded not to associate with any so-called brother or sister if that person is immoral, covetous, or an idolater, or a reviler, or a drunkard, or a swindler—and not even to eat with such a person.

Believers are free to spend time around your unbelieving friends, including those who think they are Christian but follow after false doctrines that Satan inspires. This is fellowship without expressing judgment or seeking to cause them shame. As you speak with them, be a witness for Christ and the true Gospel of Good News. You are Christ's vessel here on Earth, and perhaps he will use you to open their eyes to the truth.

From the beginning, God granted mankind dominion and power over the Earth (Genesis 1:26–28). However, through sin and deception, Satan attempted to strip mankind of that authority. But the Word of God declared that "*The lamb was slain before the foundation of this world.*" (Revelation 13:8)

Therefore, Jesus's assignment was to come all the way from Heaven to Earth to restore this lost power, giving every blood-washed, born-again believer the keys on Earth to be an overcomer of every attack from Satan and his cohorts of darkness.

God's great plan for redemption and giving us this dominus power is first accepting Jesus Christ as our Lord and Savior and allowing Him to lead us and guide us in every area of our lives. We can achieve anything by asking God through prayer and fasting. This hidden dominus power is a power that the world cannot see.

Paul talks about the veil symbolizing the difference between saints and the world or the people who do not know God. Paul says that the veil is removed when someone turns to the Lord (2 Corinthians 3:16).

I can remember when I first became filled with the Holy Ghost as I begin reading the Word of God. It was as though the Word of God came alive and began to leap off the pages into my spirit. I just began to weep because all the years I had read the Word of God, it never penetrated my heart until I was filled with the Holy Spirit. It wasn't until then that I realized the Word of God was a living soul. I remember calling my grandmother to tell her about this out-of-body experience. She was so happy for me, and she reminded me to make sure I read the Word of God every day; she repeatedly emphasized every day.

I didn't understand back then why she kept repeating "every day," but I understand it now. She knew that reading the Word every day would feed and cleanse my spirit, I would grow, and eventually I would get this dominus power from on high if I continued on this path.

"But you will receive power when the Holy Spirit comes upon you."

—Acts 1:8

The Dominus Power Empowerment of the Gifts of the Holy Spirit

Having "dominus power" in the Holy Spirit refers to the "power of the Lord" or the Holy Spirit's "supreme authority." It essentially signifies the immense, divine power bestowed upon every born-again believer through the Holy Spirit, often associated with the Greek word *dunamis*, which means "power" or "strength" in the Word of God. It describes the Holy Spirit's ability to work powerfully within individuals who submit their life to the works of Jesus Christ and allow God to transform their lives through his presence.

The *dunamis* of the Holy Spirit signifies not just a physical strength but also the capacity to perform miracles, signs, and wonders and bring about a significant change in one's life. Some of the main reasons why saints have *dunamis* given by the Holy Spirit are:

Transformation: Believers receive *dunamis* when they accept Jesus Christ, allowing them to live a life empowered by the Holy Spirit to overcome challenges and fulfill their spiritual assignment here on Earth.

Supernatural Abilities: Jesus promised His disciples that they would receive *dunamis* when the Holy Spirit came upon them, enabling them to be effective witnesses for Christ. It essentially signifies a supernatural ability to perform acts beyond human capacity, such as healing or speaking in tongues (Acts 1:8).

Believer's Impact: When a believer receives the Holy Spirit, they are empowered by *dunamis* to live a life dedicated to God, overcoming fear and daily challenges and sharing the Gospel of

Good News with holy boldness and authority with the unbelievers and the world.

Miraculous Works: The New Testament recounts numerous instances of miraculous healings, exorcisms, and other supernatural events attributed to the Holy Spirit's power.

Spiritual Gifts: The Holy Spirit bestows various spiritual gifts upon believers, such as prophecy, healing, and the ability to speak in unknown tongues, which are also manifestations of *dunamis.*

***Dunamis* and the Church:** The Holy Spirit is seen as the source of the Church's power and authority to spread the Gospel of Good News and make disciples for Christ.

***Dunamis* vs. Other Power and Sorcerers' Power:** It's important to note that *dunamis* is not simply about human strength or ability, but about God's infallible supernatural power that transcends human minds and limitations.

***Dunamis* Cannot Be Purchased by Silver or Gold:** It is not available for sale only to the rich and powerful; if it were, then millionaires and billionaires would be the only ones to receive it—the poor would not be able to afford it. You can only receive *dunamis* by being filled with the Holy Spirit. *"But you shall receive power and ability when the Holy Spirit comes upon you; and you will be My witnesses both in Jerusalem and in all Judea, and Samaria, and even to the ends of the earth."* (Acts 1:8 AMP)

GIFTS OF THE SPIRIT

Wisdom. The ability to understand God's will for your life and apply it to your daily walk. God gives us the gift of discernment along with wisdom so we can discern who is with us and who is against us among our family, friends, and new acquaintances. Satan sometimes uses those closest to us to deceive us, but, by having the wisdom of God onboard, we can see beyond the outward appearance and see the spirit that is being represented in this person.

Knowledge. Supernatural insight or revelation about specific situations or truths. God knowledge supersedes all knowledge and wisdom in the world. The God we serve is an omnipotent and omniscient God. Therefore, we can go to Him in prayer and ask Him for anything, and the Bible says He will give it to us. We can ask for knowledge and wisdom for direction in our lives and He will give it.

Faith. A strong belief in God's power and ability to work miracles. "When the enemy comes in like a flood, the Spirit of The Lord will lift up a standard against him" (Isaiah 59:19 NKJV). The Word of God declares that without faith it's impossible to please God. We must learn how to trust God in every area of our lives. The Word of God never told us to put our trust in people, or who is in power as president for a season in this nation. The Word of God instructs us to trust Him and only Him because He is a Waymaker, Miracle Worker, Promise Keeper, Light in the Darkness, Our God, that is Who He Is (Isaiah 43:19). He is The Great "I AM" God.

Healing. The gift to bring physical, emotional, or spiritual healing to others. God gives the gift of healing to represent the miracle of His healing power here on Earth to the sick and lame. God's supernatural healing takes precedence over a doctor's professional observations and science. God can and will heal miraculously by faith. God has all power in His hands.

Miracles. The ability to perform supernatural acts beyond natural laws. When we look at what is going on in our nation today, we know that it is going to take a miracle of God to turn our nation around from the bigotry, hate, and injustice that we are experiencing. We serve a God who is a miracle worker. He did it for the children of Israel when he brought them out of Egypt; if he did it back then, he can do it again. We must learn how to trust God in times like these.

Prophecy. Speaking God's message or revelation to others. *"Surely the Lord God will do nothing without revealing His secrets unto His servants the prophets"* (Amos 3:7). Many people who live in darkness everyday are unsure of God's will for their lives. They believe that the gates of Heaven are closed and they are facing this world's perils of life alone. This is far from the truth. God is speaking directly to His prophets on Earth, sharing His secrets with them of things to come.

Discerning of spirits. The ability to distinguish between the Holy Spirit's influence and other spiritual forces. Possessing this gift is one of the most important gifts you will ever possess in this life.

Through the Holy Spirit, God warns us of who to keep in our circle and who to exclude and have no fellowship.

Tongues. Speaking in a language unknown to the speaker, believed to be a gift for direct communication with God. According to the Word of God, this gift is not essential for salvation or being a Christian. It is just one of the Holy Spirit's gifts, and not all believers receive it. 1 Cor. 12:30 emphasizes that, even if you possess the gift of tongues but you lack love, this gift is useless.

Interpretation of tongues. The ability to translate the meaning of a spoken tongue into language that others understand. The Word of God instructs us that speaking in tongues should be interpreted so that the Body of Christ can be edified. Paul said that he would rather you prophesy than speak in tongues to edify the Body of Christ.

GOD CREATED YOU IN HIS IMAGE

IT IS SO IMPORTANT TODAY as we have our history books being banned across America. Satan wants the people of color to view themselves as inferior. We must teach our children and their children that they were created in God's image. The world, social media, your parents, your spouse, society, or your past mistakes do not define your Christ-like identity. God has established your identity. The Word of God declares that "God created mankind in His own image (Genesis 1:27). David affirms that we are *"fearfully and wonderfully made."* (Psalms 139:13–14)

Don't allow sin and shame to discredit or cloud your vision on how God sees you. Don't allow your shortcomings of sin to distort your understanding of your identity because your identity is hidden in Christ. When God sees you, He sees the blood.

Jesus Christ has become our advocate who intercedes for us to restore our relationship with God that was broken in the Garden of Eden. When you seek God's face daily to build a relationship with Him through our Lord and Savior Jesus Christ, we will discover and rediscover our divine purpose here on Earth, to embrace our God-given worth, and walk in the fullness of who we were created to be before the foundation of this world.

All Human Beings Were Created in God's Image. "God created all mankind in his own image; in the image of God he created them; male and female he created them." (Genesis 1:27)

God did not create human beings as animals. Some people see human beings as less than human. This is due to bigotry and hate throughout the land today. Just because someone insults you to try to make you feel less than who you was created in God's image does not mean you have to receive that negativity in your spirit. Rely on the Word of God and declare to yourself that you are what God says you are. Every human being carries God's divine image and should be treated with dignity and respect.

God Is Impartial. We serve an impartial God. He does not show favoritism or partiality based on factors like ethnicity or social status. Jesus said, "The thief comes only to steal and kill and destroy. I come that they may have life and have it more abundantly (John 10:10). Satan's tactics are for evil, not for good. There is no good within him. The Word of God declares that Satan is prowling like a roaring lion seeking someone to devour, meaning he is actively searching for people to tempt and harm, just like a lion hunts its prey.

Satan Embodies Evil and Contempt. Satan comes to divide the world, meaning that he embodies evil in many religions, seeking to create discord and conflict among people, effectively separating them and weakening their unity, often exploiting differences such as race and color, and sowing seeds of division to achieve his goals; essentially, his strategy is to divide and conquer.

Satan Uses Division as a Tactic. Satan is often depicted as using division as his primary tool to disrupt communities, societies, and even families, making it harder for people to come together and resist evil. Satan sits back and laughs when he sees that his tactics are working to divide and conquer communities, especially if he is in a position of power. The more power Satan and his cohorts of darkness have, the more they want to oppress and depress the poor and the needy. Then Peter began to speak: "I now realize how true it is that God does not show favoritism but accepts from every nation the one who fears Him and does what is right." (Acts 10:34–35)

God does not favor one race over another but judges based on faith and obedience.

Christians Must Have Unity in the Body of Christ to Eliminate Racial Divisions. Because God created humanity in his image, Christians of all races and nations must come together to show the world that we are the "Light of the World" and that there is no room for Satan's evil devices of hate and division. In Christianity, this idea is often interpreted through the Word of God where Satan is described as a deceiver who seeks to separate the people from God and from one another.

Dr. Martin Luther King, Jr. said, *"We must face the sad fact that at eleven o'clock on Sunday morning when we stand to sing 'In Christ there is no East or West,' we stand in the most segregated hour of America."*

"There is neither Jew nor Gentile, neither slave nor free, nor is there male and female, for you are all one in Christ Jesus."
—Galatians 3:28

In Christ, racial and social divisions are erased, making all believers one big spiritual family. We must reject racism and injustice and take a stand for justice in America and around the world to eliminate Satan and his cohorts of darkness from society. The Bible warns against prejudice and discrimination, urging believers to treat others fairly.

"My brothers and sisters, believers in our glorious Lord Jesus Christ must not show favoritism."
—James 2:1 (NIV)

Jesus Confronted Racial Prejudice. God has given us real life and real-world examples today by taking a look at our politics. Our leaders are canceling diversity, equity, and inclusion in hopes of having an economic impact on a certain ethnic group of people because they are in power and control.

They have no idea that we serve a God of justice, and He has created all humanity in His image because they have no fear of Him. Satan's desire is to sow division and discord among God's people by pitting them against each other based on race, politics, or other societal divisions, which can be seen as tactics used by malicious bad actors to manipulate and control. Jesus spoke with the Samaritan woman despite cultural and racial animosity, demonstrating that God's love transcends human divisions (John 4:9).

Heaven Will Be Filled With Every Nation and All People: "For God so loved the world that He gave His only begotten Son, that whosoever believeth in Him should not perish, but have eternal life."
—John 3:16

No blood-washed, born-again believers should live with hate and bigotry in their hearts. If they claim to be Christians, they must not judge others based on their physical appearance, color, nationality, or ethnicity. People look at the outer appearance, but God looks at the heart. Loving your neighbor is the second greatest commandment from our Lord and Savior Jesus Christ. The first commandment states, *"You shall love the Lord your God with all your heart, with all your soul, with all your strength, and with all your mind,' and second in command he said "You shall love your neighbor, as yourself."* (Luke 10:25–37)

If you say you love God and hate your neighbor, then you don't have the love of God within you. Furthermore, you cannot make it to Heaven with hate or bigotry in your heart. The Word of God declares in the Book of Revelation that *"After this I looked, and there before me was a great multitude that no one could count, from every nation, tribe, people and language, standing before the throne and before the Lamb. They were wearing white robes and were holding palm branches in their hands."* (Revelation 7:9)

PART

II

Satan Is the Father of Lies

Satan Is the Prince of Darkness

SATAN IS THE CHIEF OF EVIL, LIES, AND DECEPTION, and he is a murderer. Satan is described as having power over some illnesses, death, and some people. Satan can deceive millions here on Earth at one time. He uses people closest to you to deceive you. The kingdom of darkness is well equipped and ready to fight us each day. Satan will use any available vessel at his disposal. Satan has organized and trained his team to be on his assignments and command. Sometimes, when Satan and his cohorts of darkness are traveling throughout the Earth, they are searching and looking for disruptive signs, such as arguments, hatred, and resentment. Sometimes, interpretations suggest that Satan seeks to enter people's lives through gates or open doors, such as sin, unforgiveness of the heart, and a lack of faith.

Satan will show up uninvited to the table, even though this house was not on his original assignment. He hears the disruption, which allows him to enter through certain spiritual gates. The next thing you know, the demons of anger have entered the conversation of the human vessels, and the chain of events happens so quickly, sometimes within a matter of seconds. The angry spirit takes control of the mind and encourages the human vessel Satan entered to shoot to kill, and someone gets shot dead. Sometimes, two demons show up simultaneously, rolling together—they are referred to as the murder and suicide demons.

The murder demons murder everything in the house, including the children and animals; then the suicide demons step in and encourage the murderer to shoot themselves. Satan then exits the house or the scene because his command assignment for murdering this family has been accomplished. Satan retreats and laughs at the human who committed the murders without recognizing Satan's spirit, not realizing that Satan only showed up for their demise. Satan then continues traveling throughout the Earth in his extraterrestrial body to find his next human victim(s) living in sin and darkness to deceive and conquer.

Some of the descriptions of Satan and his kingdom of darkness are noted below. Satan's desire is for humanity to ignore him and his existence; some people don't believe there are such things as Satan and his demons or cohorts of darkness operating daily on Earth, even though they see murders and killings occurring every day. They believe that it was just a bad actor who carried out bad acts. The Word of God declares that we are wrestling with spiritual warfare; there is a battle going on between the Kingdom of God and the kingdom of darkness. It's an ongoing internal and external struggle against God's enemies.

Spiritual Wickedness in High Places

These spirits are high-ranking officers in the spirit realm that have been assigned specialized jurisdictions over the cosmological systems of the universe and rule in the kingdom of darkness. They are responsible for blinding people's minds to the truth of God's Word and implementing sin, wickedness, evil, and iniquity on Earth. These demons are responsible for keeping the unsaved folks in darkness in the world today. When we speak about darkness, we refer to the difference of the saved folks walking in the light and the unsaved walking in darkness because they cannot see in the spirit realm. Jesus said, *"I am the light of the world. No one who follows me stumbles around in the darkness. I provide plenty of light to live in. He who follows me shall not walk in darkness but have the light of life."* (John 8:12)

Jesus gives us not only light but also his divine revelations to see those things that are unseen. These cosmological demons affect our thoughts, feelings, and perceptions of humanity through social media, music, fashion, sports, philosophies, and religious ideologies.

Principalities

The word Greek word for principality is *archomai*, which means "first in rank order." Principalities derive their power from Satan himself and are known to be the highest-ranking in Satan's army. They influence all human affairs at the national level, impacting laws and policies. These demonic forces are recognizable today in our nation and in other political arenas. They are purpose-driven demons and warlocks, and they usually embody world leaders. There were principalities of evil and darkness operating in Adolf Hitler, when we examine how he was on an assignment to murder the Jews. Hitler's primary goal was to establish a racially pure German state, known as the Third Reich, by expanding German territory through military conquest, eliminating the Jews and other groups that Nazi ideology considered marginalized and inferior, and dominating Europe with the Aryan race as the superior power, all while seeking to overturn the restrictions imposed on Germany by the Treaty of Versailles after World War I.

Hitler's Desire was to Establish Germany as the Dominant Power in Germany, subjugating other nations. The Nazi Party committed mass murder on an unprecedented scale. The Nazis and their allies collaborated to kill over six million Jews through systematic, state-sponsored genocide, which is now known as the Holocaust.

When We Look Back Over the History of America, the African American was stolen from their homeland of Africa and sold into slavery. They have endured so many injustices based solely on the color of their skin, and they are still enduring racial inequities and injustices as a people of color today, even though God created them in His image. There is only one race—the human race. However, Satan's evil spirit of division wants to divide, conquer, and enslave the other races based solely on their color, just as the Nazis did during World War II.

Satan and his cohorts of darkness sometimes disguise themselves as Christians (angels of light); these are the demons Christ spoke about when He acknowledged they are demons from hell and not of God. They are a part of Satan's kingdom of darkness; they don't know or understand that God created all people equal and in His image.

Powers Are Next in Command

The Greek word for power is *exousia* and refers to delegated authority. These demons of darkness drive their jurisdiction and delegate authority from the principalities of darkness. They affect and infect structures, systems, and the five pillars of our society: marriage, family, government, education, and the house of God.

Demons and Warlocks

The Greek word *daimonion* means "distributor of fortunes." Demons and warlocks in the supernatural spirit that possess the nature of Satan and his demons have the ability to give and distribute fortunes. "Mammon of the unrighteous" possess humanity and control their mindsets and activities. Demons and warlocks can be worshipped, make people sick, communicate with the dead, and involve themselves in a host of other evil and diabolic activities that Satan encourages.

Familiar Spirits

They are supernatural entities that can take the form of animals, humans, imps, or fairies. They are also known as familiars, animal familiars, or spirit guides.

Beliefs about Familiar Spirits:

- Some cultures believe familiar spirits provide magical ability, guidance, protection, or healing.
- The Bible uses the term "familiar spirit" to refer to demons that are close to or familiar with a person.
- The Bible warns against consulting with mediums and spiritists, who are said to have familiar spirits.

Some Ways Familiar Spirits Enter into Human Vessels:

- Divination
- Transcendental meditation
- New Age visualization
- Necromancy
- Witchcraft
- Drugs and alcohol

Satan's Kingdom of Darkness Is Any Territory or Domain Where God Is Not Present

Satan reigns when there is no spiritual or divine revelation, purpose, and known presence of God, where spiritual blindness can be manipulated and used as mass destruction. This gives Satan the power to invade territories where he is unwelcome. Satan knows that if a person doesn't know God, they are in the dark and blind to his evil plots and plans to destroy them through deception. Satan wants to see their eventual total demise (death).

This is why Satan is going to and fro throughout the Earth, lying, deceiving, and killing those who have chosen to follow the prince of darkness rather than the God of Light. The kingdom of darkness is equipped to fight us in battle by any means necessary. We are facing a very organized system.

Satan Operates in Deception

Satan uses deception because he dwells in the dark, but if you are walking in the light in the presence of the Lord, you should be able to discern when you are entertaining Satan's deceptive spirit among people, especially in relationships. You may have trusted someone because of their appearance or smooth, seductive words, and now you have learned that you were deceived. Satan was operating in their flesh. Satan, who is *"...the god of this world has blinded the minds of unbelievers, so that they cannot see the glorious light of the gospel that displays the glory of Christ, who is the exact image of God."* (2 Corinthians 4:4)

Saints Must Take Back Their Power from Satan

Remember that Satan will always need a human body (flesh and blood) to carry out his evil assignments here on Earth. Satan is God's chief adversary, so he hates Christians who are believers and followers of Christ. Satan is referred to as the "prince of darkness" because he transforms himself into an "angel of light" to deceive the weak and the feeble-minded. Satan is the father of lies. *"You are of your father the devil, and your will is to do your father's desires. He was a murderer from the beginning, and there is no truth in him. When he lies, he speaks according to his own nature, for he is a liar and the father of lies."* (John 8:44)

SATAN GASLIGHTS AND MANIPULATES THE WEAK AND THE FEEBLE

SATAN MANIPULATED EVE in the Garden of Eden when he tempted her to eat the fruit of the forbidden tree. Satan entered the snake to deceive Eve while Adam was away feeding the animals in the garden. This is one of Satan's greatest tools; he seeks to seduce and deceive you when you are alone. Satan deceived Eve by lying to her, telling her that if she ate the forbidden fruit she would be like God. "Then the serpent said to the woman, *"You will not surely die. For God knows that when you eat from it your eyes will be opened, and you will be like God, knowing good and evil."* (Genesis 3:4)

Consequences for Deception and Confusion

The Word of God tells us that Adam and Eve were both punished, banished from the Garden of Eden, and condemned to a life of hardship. These were the consequences for their eating the forbidden fruit from the Tree of Knowledge of Good and Evil:

- Adam cursed the ground, which would now produce thorns and thistles.
- God condemned humans to eat plants of the field through painful toil.
- God alienated Eve alienated from her man, alienated her from her maternal body, and alienated her from Him, and He condemned all women to pain in childbirth.

Other Consequences

Humanity was cursed with toil, disease, and death; humanity fell from what was called original innocence to sin and shame. These are just some of the consequences of walking in disobedience to God's word and instruction. When we allow Satan to come into our daily lives and seduce us to turn away from God's will and word, we must pay the consequences. Satan is still deceiving millions every day to follow him and not the Word of God.

Satan Is the Enemy of God and Christ: The Prince of Evil Spirits Satan Opposes Everything That Is Holy

ACCORDING TO THE WORD OF GOD, Satan, the world, the flesh, and those who are alienated from God are God's enemies. Satan was a fallen angel who thought he was equal to God; his pride and arrogance led his being extradited from Heaven and becoming God's chief adversary here on Earth.

We Are in a Spiritual Battle

The world we live in represents this battle every day. There are wars and rumors of war; murder, child molestations, hate, and bigotry are rampant in our nation; it's all spiritual warfare. The injustices that are currently being practiced and put into law against people of color and marginalized communities are evidence that in these times of uncertainty we must trust God even more. Satan's spirit of deception and moral corruption is running rapid throughout the land. We as blood-washed, born-again believers must recognize that our fight is not against flesh and blood but against spiritual wickedness in high places.

Real-Life Application

The world reflects this spiritual battle—wars, injustices, moral decay, and deception. Believers must recognize that their fight is not against flesh and blood but against spiritual forces (Ephesians 6:12). Through prayer, fasting, and standing firm in God's Word, we can resist the darkness.

Saints Have to Take Spiritual Authority Over Satan

"Finally, my brethren, be strong in the Lord and in the power of His might. Put on the whole armor of God, so that you may be able to stand against the wiles of the devil. For we do not wrestle against flesh and blood, but against principalities, against powers, against the rulers of the darkness of this age, against spiritual hosts of wickedness in the heavenly places. Therefore, take up the whole armor of God, so that you may be able to withstand in the evil day, and having done all, to stand."

—Ephesians 6:10–13

Even Though God Created Humanity in His Image, humanity chose to worship the creature over their creator. The Word of God in Romans 1:25 says that people have chosen to worship the creation over the Creator. This means that they have traded the truth about God and chose to worship Satan and his lies and deception. This has created the world to be an enemy of God. When we see a

34-time convicted felon serving in the highest office in the land, we can see where millions have been blinded and deceived and chose to worship the creature over the creator. They have chosen to worship the father of lies and his cohorts of darkness going throughout the Earth.

People have rejected the truth of the Word of God and chosen to believe Satan's lies and deception. They have worshipped things that God created, such as idols made to look like people, animals, and birds. They have chosen to worship these things. They have dishonored their bodies by engaging in shameful acts with each other.

"Stay alert! Watch out for your great enemy, the devil. He prowls like a roaring lion, looking for someone to devour. Stand firm against him and be strong in your faith. Remember that your family of believers all over the world is going through the same kind of suffering you are."
—1 Peter 5:8–9 (NLT)

There Is Spiritual Warfare Between Good and Evil

Satan is a liar and an imposter. When God aborted his illegal takeover in Heaven, Satan is now taking over the Earth by using his terrestrial body to invade humans to accomplish his evil and wicked assignments.

Satan Thrown Out of Heaven

Satan tried to usurp authority over God. "And war broke out in heaven: Michael and his angels fought with the dragon; and the dragon and his angels fought, but they did not prevail, nor was a place found for them in heaven any longer. So the great dragon was cast out, that serpent of old, called the Devil and Satan, who deceives the whole world; he was cast to the earth, and his angels were cast out with him." (Revelation 12:7–9)

Satan's and His Cohorts of Darkness Rebel Against God

The Word of God describes Satan as Lucifer being cast down from Heaven due to his pride and desire to take over the kingdom of Heaven and usurp authority over God (Isaiah 14:12–15). The Word of God declares that pride goes before a fall. We can see today in this nation that we have leaders in authority walking in pride and deception, which represents Satan occupying their vessels here on Earth. Pride and rebellion against God's laws and commandments here on Earth are always a recipe for failure. Just as Satan fell because of his pride and arrogance, humanity falls spiritually when it magnifies and glorifies themselves and ignores humility and submission to God. God's Word cannot fail.

"I am not a man that I would lie to you;
neither am I the son of man that I would have to repent."
—Numbers 23:19

Satan and his cohorts of darkness have the power to oppress, possess, and terrorize the poor and the needy. Satan uses those that are in position and power to oppress the poor. The Word of God declares,

"He who oppresses the poor to increase his riches, and he who gives to the rich, will surely come to poverty." (Proverbs 22:16)

Whoever oppresses the poor shows contempt for their Maker, but whoever is kind to the needy honors God. How we treat the poor and needy says a lot about our heart. There is one thing God is very clear about throughout His Word: He desires for us to care for the poor and the needy among us. Scripture says, *"He who is gracious and lends a hand to the poor lends to the Lord, and the Lord will repay him for his good deed."* (Proverbs 19:17 AMP)

You have the authority of Christ over Satan and his demons. You have been given authority over Satan in the spirit realm. You were once lost, but now you are found. You must take your inheritance in the kingdom of God. Satan no longer has the victory over your life. God has brought you out of darkness into his glorious light. Paul said, *"You were dead because of your sins and because your sinful nature was not yet cut away. Then God made you alive with Christ, for he forgave all our sins. He canceled the record of the charges against us and took it away by nailing it to the cross. In this way, he disarmed the spiritual rulers and authorities. He shamed them publicly by his victory over them on the cross."* (2 Colossians 2:13–15 NLT)

Satan Transforms Himself as an Angel of Light

PAUL PROTECTS THE CHRISTIANS IN CORINTH, comparing them to a betrothed bride and himself to her father. He warns them that the false apostles are trying to seduce the Corinthians away from their belief and commitment to Christ.

Satan can Transform Himself as an Apostle, Prophet, Pastor, Preacher, Priest, Bishop, or any other leader to deceive others who do not know God and walk in darkness. Satan is the father of lies, so he needs to represent something that he is not to carry out his evil works here on Earth.

Satan is here illegally; therefore, Satan has a terrestrial body (spiritual being) that never rests; he will need to possess a human body (flesh and blood) to carry out his evil acts on Earth. So Satan travels throughout the Earth looking to see who he can deceive and devour. Satan is looking for a dry place. The appearance of this person may be pleasant to look upon, they can be the president or king of a nation or hold the highest position in the land in politics, or they can be a leader of the clergy, they can a family member, they can be a child, they can be a parent, they can friend, or they can be a spouse; but they are on Satan's assignment. They have chosen and submitted to serve Satan to do evil and not good to represent God.

"And the Lord said to Satan, From where do you come?
Satan answered the Lord and said,
'From going to and fro on the earth,
and from walking back and forth on it.'"
—Job 1:7

This remarkable heavenly scene provides an amazing snippet of demonic activity. In opposition to God and His provision of salvation, the devil apparently never rests and is the exact opposite. He's NOT omnipresent, as God is, because he has a finite mind, unlike God's infinite mind. God created this evil being and removed him from Heaven and has allowed him on Earth for a season.

Satan time is limited here on Earth, therefore, he has limited time to accomplish his evil works on Earth. It seems that the devil continues from place to place, perfecting his deceptions and using as many people who walk in darkness as are willing to be his prime candidates to be possessed and influenced to carry out his evil assignment. He doesn't seem to have a shortage of willing accomplices. I'm sure that if he does take a break, he must have assigned his cohorts of darkness to the second and third shifts because it seems like the Earth never gets a break!

Therefore, God urgently warns us: *"Be sober, be vigilant, because your adversary the devil walks about like a roaring lion, seeking whom he may devour."* (1 Peter 5:8)

The evil angels who rebelled against God also seem never to

rest until they can take possession of someone's mind to manipulate and control their behavior.

"When an Unclean Spirit Goes Out of a Man, it goes through dry places, seeking rest, and finds none. Then it says, 'I will return to my house from which I came.' When it arrives, it finds the house unoccupied, swept clean and put in order."
—Mathew 12:43–44

Satan is seeking to find the person who had once received salvation and living for Christ; but something happened on their Christian journey, and they lost hope and fell into a backslidden condition. The heavy weight of sin, guilt, and trying to come out sometimes causes many to end their lives when repentance was just a prayer away.

Satan seeks to reoccupy that person or repossess them to carry out his acts of evil and wickedness. There is a restlessness in the souls of unsaved individuals that seems to mirror Satan's restlessness and that of his cohorts of darkness. We should expect that from those who join Satan's evil agenda we see all around us.

"They have no rest day or night,
who worship the beast and his image,
and whoever receives the mark of his name."
—Revelation 14:11

True Rest for Our Souls Can Only be Found in Jesus Christ with His forgiveness, cleansing, and guidance: *"Come to me, all you who labor and are heavy laden, and I will give you rest. Take my yoke upon you and learn from me, for I am gentle and lowly in heart, and you will find rest for your souls."* (Matthew 11:28–29)

Paul compares false Apostles to serpents who tempt people away from their commitment to Christ. Paul warns that Satan's greatest weapon is deception, and that the most effective deception is to convince people that evil is good and darkness is light. *"And no wonder, for even Satan disguises himself as an angel of light." (2 Corinthians 11:14)*

PART

III

Pray for God to open Your Eyes to See Satan and His Co-Horts of Darkness

Building a Foundational Relationship With Jesus Christ

JESUS CHRIST IS THE CHIEF CORNERSTONE OF OUR FAITH. "For no one can lay any foundation other than the one already laid, which is Jesus Christ. Now, if anyone builds on this foundation using gold, silver, precious stones, wood, hay, or straw, their work will be shown for what it is because the day will bring it to light. It will be revealed with fire, and the fire will test the quality of each person's work. If what has been built survives, the builder will receive a reward. If it is burned up, the builder will suffer loss yet will be saved—even though only as one escaping through the flames. Don't you know that you yourselves are God's temple and that God's spirit dwells in you? If anyone destroys God's temple, God will destroy that person, for God's temple is sacred, and you together are that temple." (1 Corinthians 3:11–17)

You were built on the foundation laid by apostles and prophets with Jesus Christ himself being the cornerstone. In him, every act of building, of being connected, causes growth into the holy temple in the Lord. In him, you too are being built together into a dwelling place for God by the Holy Spirit.

Building a firm foundation requires faith. Building a firm foundation in Christ requires patience, tenacity, and, above all, faith. The Word of God declares that "without faith it is impossible to please God because anyone who comes to him must believe that He exists and that He rewards those who earnestly seek Him" (Hebrews 11:6). If we are to anticipate joyfully, adhere continually, and adore increasingly, proper faith is necessary; faith that is not ourselves or in the things that we do, but in Christ alone.

Prayer is a strong foundation of faith. It is essential to cultivating a sound relationship with the Almighty Omnipotent God, fostering spiritual growth and understanding through communication and seeking daily guidance. Prayer for building a strong foundation in Christ Jesus.

"Dear Lord, thank you for your words of wisdom and guidance. Lord, please help me to not only hear your words; but help me to be a doer to put them into action to see transformation in my daily walk. Help me to be like the wise man who built his house on a rock, with a strong foundation in you and not the world. In Jesus Name Amen."

Why is Prayer important to a Believer?

It's Direct Communication with Jesus Christ.

Prayer allows individuals to engage in a two-way conversation with our Lord and Savior Jesus Christ, who is our intercessor with God, expressing our needs, seeking daily guidance, and experiencing God's presence while waiting patiently for Him to answer our prayers and meet all of our needs.

Prayer Strengthens Our Faith in God.

Having a consistent prayer life for saints deepens our faith in God to trust Him more. Learning how to recognize His voice is one of the key elements to building a strong prayer life. The Word of God declares that *"The effectual fervent prayer of a righteous man availeth much"* (James 5:16), meaning that a sincere and passionate prayer from a righteous person has great power and can accomplish a lot.

Prayer Enhances Our Spiritual Growth.

Prayer is the vehicle for spiritual growth and development, helping believers to understand God's will and align their lives with His divine purpose and the plans He has designed for them before the foundation of this world.

Prayer Is Seeking Divine Intervention.

Prayer is seeking divine intervention for God to intervene in our personal life, our relationships, and the lives of others, aligning with God's will and inviting His power to work in the world. Prayer can help saints overcome daily challenges that Satan and his cohorts of darkness use to attack us; prayer gives us the strength to become overcomers and to persevere and navigate through life's turmoil and difficult times.

Prayer Activates Our Faith.

Prayer itself is an act of faith because it involves believing in the unseen and involves believing in God's existence, power, and willingness to hear our voice and answer our prayers when we humble ourselves before the Lord. God hears our prayers.

Prayer Is for Confession and Repentance.

Prayer provides an opportunity for confession and seeking forgiveness, leading to spiritual renewal and growth.

Trusting God to Be Your Light in Darkness and Jehovah Jireh in Your Life

The Lord God Is Your Light and Your Salvation

David constantly experienced many battles with Satan and his cohorts of darkness. David wrote many psalms to encourage himself in the Lord. Sometimes when we go through trials and tribulations, when we get weak in our flesh, and it seems like we are not going to make it, and we are all alone, this is Satan speaking to your mind. God promised us that He would dwell in a thick cloud (2 Chronicles 6:1), meaning that when you cannot see your way through, God will see you through.

He promised us in his Word that he will never leave us or forsake us. His name is Jehovah El Roi; he is the God who sees me! This is the time to get into the Word of God and let it minister to your heart so you can come alive again to live your best life. We must take on the unshakable, unmovable faith of David when he said "The Lord is my Light and my Salvation; whom shall I fear? The LORD is the STRENGTH of my life; of whom shall I be afraid?" (Psalms 27:1)

David made a decision to take his life back from Satan when he was trying to make him walk in fear and anxiety. We must learn that God is the author and finisher of our faith. Every time Satan comes in and has you feeling hopeless and uncertain due to your circumstances, pray and stand on the Word of God and his promises. God illuminates our path and removes confusion, leading and guiding us through every dark season. Believe it! Receive it! Walk in it!

God Is Our Jehovah Jireh

The name Jehovah Jireh means "The Lord will provide." Just as God provided a ram for Abraham in the place of Isaac, He is here and ready to meet you and me at the point of our needs (Genesis 22:14).

I will never forget when I moved from Savannah to Atlanta over 40 years ago. I left an extremely abusive marriage, and I felt as though I couldn't live this life of fear and anxiety anymore. When I moved to Atlanta, I had no job, no place to stay, and no friends. But I had a whole lot of faith and didn't even know it, and guess what: my God did provide. He gave me shelter that night with a bunch of women with whom I had a lot in common; God gave me a job within three weeks, and the rest is history.

But what I didn't know, which was the most important aspect of my journey, was that God had ordered my steps to Atlanta for me to get to the feet of Jesus—the best decision I ever made. When I met Christ for the very first time, I felt a radical internal transformation, and I fell deeply in love with the lover of my soul. I am a living witness and testament to the Word of God: "My God shall supply all of my needs according to His riches and glory in

Christ Jesus" (Philippians 4:19). Ever since that day, I can honestly say he has repeatedly taken care of me. We must learn to trust God for every area of our lives, God will make provisions for our finances, our relationships, our health, and our spiritual growth fosters peace and contentment, knowing that God is always faithful.

Marriage Was Designed for Christian Relationships

SATAN ATTACKS CHRISTIANS and deceives them about dating and marriage because he seeks to distort God's word for Christian relationships and prevent believers from trusting God's plans for their lives and His will for marriage. Here are some key reasons why we must have a serious prayer life, be vigilant, allow the spirit of discernment to permeate our being, and ask God to show us whatever Satan might be hiding in darkness if someone is on Satan's assignment to deceive you and disrupt your life.

This generation in the dating world need to hear the voice of God more today than ever because Satan knows how to transform himself as your angel of light to get you caught up into his ether and web of deception. The Word of God says, do not adjoined together with unbelievers.

God Created Godly Relationships from the Beginning in the Garden of Eden between Adam and Eve. God created them for His glory and to have a personal relationship with them, and to reflect on his image here on Earth. Essentially, to create human beings capable of love and fellowship with Him. Their story highlights the importance of companionship by God's creating Eve as a "helper" for Adam, not leaving Adam alone. This is why men and women thirst for companionship and desire to be in healthy relationships today and do not like to be alone.

Companionship. God saw that it did Adam no good to be alone, so he created Eve as a suitable partner. This is why men and women today desire to be in a marriage to give God glory. The Word of God declares that *"Marriage is honorable in all, and the bed undefiled; but whoremongers and adulterers God will judge."* (Hebrews 13:4)

Celibacy is Important in Christian Dating. Abstaining from sex until marriage (yes in 2025) is crucial in your Christian walk and aligns with God's design for Christian relationships. Paul reminded the disciples: *"Present your bodies as a living sacrifice, holy and acceptable to God, which is your spiritual worship."* (Romans 12:1)

Why does this matter? Because it protects your spirit and emotional well-being and strengthens faith and self-control.

Free Will. God gave Adam and Eve the ability to choose, represented by the Tree of Knowledge of Good and Evil, allowing them to decide to follow His commands. You still must choose the kind of person you allow into your closed space. If you listen to the person's conversion and they don't sound God-fearing, please don't allow them into your space. Sometimes you know right away. Keep it moving; don't give an ear to Satan because he will take more than you have to give.

We Must Learn to Obey God's Commands. The Word of God declares that sexual intimacy is reserved for marriage (Hebrews 13:4). 1 Cor. 6:18–20 warns us to flee from sexual immorality because our bodies are the temple of the Holy Spirit. Celibacy honors God and demonstrates how strong our relationship is with Him and how faithful we are to keeping His commandments.

Celibacy Protects Our Emotions and Spiritual Health. Sexual intimacy creates a deep spiritual bond between a man and a woman. Genesis 2:24 speaks of a man uniting with his wife, and the two shall become one flesh. Every time you lie down with someone, you become one with them, and you have created a soul tie. The woman has literally put someone in a husband's position who was not her husband. This is why you continue to yearn for this person, even though the two of you were not married. This is one of the curses of Eve after the fall in the garden: *"Your desire shall be for your husband, and he shall rule over you."* (Genesis. 3:16)

Christian couples who practice celibacy during their courtship develop better relationship communication and trust because their relationship is based on getting to know each other during their courtship phase. As a Christian couple you are not clouded with fleshly activity, and you get to see the person's true Christian character. It shows discipline and that your walk with God is more authentic then being tempted with worldly temptations. You must learn to set boundaries, be mindful of environments that could lead to temptations, and surround yourselves with like-minded friends.

The Word of God states that humans are created in God's image, signifying a special connection and love between Him and humanity.

God created Christian relationships for marriage and reproduction on Earth to reflect His love and establish His covenant as mentioned in the Word of God. *"For this reason, a man shall leave his father and mother and be joined to his wife, and the two shall become one flesh."* (Ephesians 5:31–32)

God's original plan for marriage was for one man and one woman in a lifelong relationship. God's desire was for the Earth to be filled with people who would share His image and have dominion over creation, fulfilling a divine plan for humanity to cultivate and govern the Earth.

Marriage is a powerful tool to represent Christ and the Church. Satan seeks to corrupt, destroy, or pervert our Christian relationships today before they even reach that stage by sending his cohorts of darkness to deceive and destroy Christians. Satan's desire is for humanity to live in ungodly relationships and to take away the glory of God and His plans for humanity to multiply on Earth. This is why Paul said to the church, *"Do not be unequally yoked with unbelievers."* (Corinthians 6:14)

He followed this imperative with a series of five questions used to draw contrast, such as *"For what partnership has righteousness with lawlessness?"* or *"What fellowship has light with darkness?"*

Satan and his cohorts of darkness invade the Christian dating world today by transforming themselves as "angels of light" to deceive the believers. *"For there shall arise false Christs, and false prophets, and shall shew great signs and wonders; insomuch that, if it were possible, they shall deceive the very elect."*

Satan and his cohorts of darkness have invaded our churches, social media, Christian dating sites, Christian groups, and other platforms where fellowshipping to find like-minded Christians usually occurs. Their assignment is to lie, seduce, and deceive. They come into believers' lives to rob, steal, or murder them. Satan and his cohorts of darkness are the father of lies—the truth is not in them.

Their desire to see their prey's demise was always present from day one because they walk in darkness. Sometimes they will even marry their prey to accomplish their evil assignments of destruction. This is why it is so important to be filled with the Holy Spirit, to be discerning, and to have a fervent prayer life.

I have counseled and coached many Christians about their relationships or marriages that they may have been in for years, sometimes decades. They say things like "he likes men, and we were married for 20+ years, and he divorced me for a man," or "he said he owned several businesses, and he needed my money to get his business off the ground because his money was tied up for the time being."

"For God So Loved the World That He Gave His Only Son, that whoever believes in him should not perish but have eternal life."
—John 3:16

Pray and ask God for the spirit of discernment. Is this the right person for you? Sometimes there are several red flags. Here are just a few:

- The word of God declares that Love is not just a feeling: *"Charity suffereth long, and is kind, charity envieth not, charity vaunted not itself, it is not puffed up, doth not behave itself unseemly, seeketh not her own, is not easily provoked, thinketh no evil, rejoiceth not in iniquity, but rejoiceth in the truth; beareth all things, believeth all things, hopeth all things, endureth all things." Love is patient, kind, and selfless—not envious or boastful; love endures through difficulties and always sees the best for others."* (1 Corinthians 13:4–7)

- They don't have a genuine relationship with God. They claimed that they had a relationship with God when you first began dating and attended church with you on several occasions, but now they don't have time to attend church, or they find an excuse not to attend church with you or pray with you, or they say that you might be too spiritual for them.
- They pressure you to compromise your faith and lifestyle. They tell you that every Christian is doing this in the church today; they question your Christian faith and commitment to a lifestyle of celibacy before marriage; they try to mock you or question whether your commitment to Christ is real and try to imply that it's impossible to live your lifestyle.
- They don't encourage your spiritual growth. They don't have a prayer life and don't want you to have one. They may tell you that you are too spiritual for them or try to discourage your everyday walk with Christ by saying there are no perfect Christians here on Earth. They want to party and go clubbing and tell you that there's nothing wrong with Christians having a little fun in life. They try to tell you that Jesus would understand because his first miracle was at a wedding where he turned the water into wine to

have fun. *"They have a form of godliness but deny its power. And from such people turn away."* (2 Timothy 3:5)

- Please flee from these types of Christians, and don't allow them to gaslight or manipulate your relationship with Christ.
- You have been dating for three to four months and they never invite you to their place but always want to hang out at your place. They never want to take you out to a restaurant. They always come up with an excuse. Sometimes they are hiding something negative, such as living with their parents or living with another woman or man. Sometimes they may even be married.
- They are living in down-low relationships. Satan uses some men to disguise themselves as "angels of light." These men are sometimes leaders in the church or grew up in the church, and some leader they trusted in the church molested them during their adolescence in the church. They are faithful to their church assignments. Some may look extremely masculine with no trace of femininity, but they love to have relationships with random men that they meet in the church or at church conventions, clubs, gyms, etc., or they may be in a long-term relationship with their college frat brother who understands their choice to date women as well. It may be an old army buddy, as long he understands that he is the only man involved in their open relationship.

They are trying to find a lonely woman of God who desires to get married and have children before a certain age. They love to have children and a family to put on a good front for their families and the church. The woman is usually referred as a "beard" in their lives. This is another reason why you really need to be filled with the Holy Ghost, also known as the "Spirit of Truth," because *"When he, the Spirit of truth, comes, he will guide you into all the truth. He will not speak on his own; he will speak only what he hears, and he will tell you what is yet to come."* (John 16:13)

There are too many first ladies writing books today about their life stories of being married to down-low men for 10+ years.

- They may pay for the first few dates to seduce you and hope that you get caught up in their ether. Now their money is funny. It is tied up in some business venture, and they want you to foot the bill.
- They never talk about their family or about introducing you to their children or family. If family is important to you, then you don't want to marry someone who does not respect their parents or doesn't get along with family members. They have only negative or derogatory things to say about family. These are warning signs of their inability to communicate with others.
- Get out of dead relationships. You have been in a relationship for two, five, or 10+ years, and they still have no intentions or conversations about getting married to you, especially if you are 40+. Most people have figured out by now who they are and what type of person they would like to share their lives with. These people are called "blockers"—they don't want you, and they don't want anyone else to have you. These are called "friends with

benefits relationships" because you haven't required more from the relationship. They gaslight and manipulate you emotionally and mentally to keep you in bondage and try to tell you that you all have something special that is real love; but it's not. They may even refer to you often as "wifey." Love is an action word that emphasizes love is not just a feeling—you demonstrate it through actions of caring, commitment, and support. If you never went to the justice of the peace, you are not married.

This same person will leave you and marry someone else in less than three months because they feel as though they finally found out and know what real love is. While being in this dead relationship with you, they choose to continue in it to keep their options open and play the field. Sometimes these people may be in the church and serving as leaders and just keep stringing you along because they feel as though they have too many available options.

- Satan Wants to Undermine Godly Relationships. God designed godly relationships for marriage to reflect his covenant from the beginning in the Garden of Eden. Because marriage is a powerful tool and solid representation of our Lord and Savior Jesus Christ and the church, it will always be under attack from Satan, whose desire is to destroy the foundation of marriage as God intended from the beginning. This is why he produces perverted relationships today to stop establishment of the family and reproduction of children. Marriage between a man and a woman represents God and his original plan for humanity.

- Satan uses temptation to distract us. Satan tempts Christian couples to engage in premarital sex, violating God's plan for purity. Satan deceives them into believing that certain sins are forgivable, and all they must do is repent and get back up, and God will forgive them. It is so important that you connect with someone who shares your same spiritual goals and beliefs because many Christians falsely profess that they possess the Holy Spirit. Satan and his cohorts of darkness will try to tell you that some sins aren't really a big deal to weaken your walk and commitment to Christ because they don't have that kind of commitment.
- *"Beware of Dogs, those Evildoers, those Mutilators of the Flesh."* Paul's warning in Philippians 3:2 isn't literally about the animal but about the false teachers who promote legalistic religious practices. He uses the term "dogs" as a derogatory term for those who reject the Gospel and instead cling to their old sinful ways. God has given me dreams and visions of people in my life or people who were trying to get into my life, but they were dogs. I know that he was warning me about those who claimed to be Christian but who may have had a different doctrine or never met Christ. I recall meeting a pastor who was ordained in the Church of God in Christ; he was elated to present his ordination papers to show me that he was a pastor. When I went to bed that night, God brought the pastor before me in a revelation and revealed to me that this pastor had a spirit of "perversion." I didn't initially know what kind of perversion he had, but God did warn me, so, I was vigilant and just listened to the pastor talk, and it eventually came out.

Because we worked together on the same job, I was able to speak with him on several occasions and observed that he did indeed have a "perverted spirit" and was probably one of those that Christ spoke of when He said, *"Many will say to Me in that day, 'Lord, Lord, have we not prophesied in Your name, cast out demons in Your name, and done many wonders in Your name?' And then I will declare to them, 'I never knew you; depart from Me, you who practice lawlessness.'"* (Matthew 7:22–23)

Many Christians fall into a deceptive relationship because it appears to be good on the outside; however, the more they get involved in the relationship, the more it begins to lead them away from God's purpose for their lives.

- Satan will send a camouflage. Many Christians fall into relationships that may seems a good fit at first. The two of you may have a lot in common, and you have finally met the partner of your dreams. God has finally sent you your Boaz, so you thought. Satan will transform himself as an "angel of light" especially in a new relationship. He showers you with flowers, expensive gifts, and fine dining restaurants. Satan desires to sweep you off your feet to give you a sense of false peace and emotional excitement, if there were any "red flags" in your partner's character that the "Holy Spirit" was warning you about. But you ignored them because you were in denial. Satan has sent you the wrong person at the right time because he knows what you were going through.

This may be a challenging time in your life where you are most vulnerable. You may have just gone through a divorce or bereavement such as the loss of a child, parent, or sibling. Satan knows when you are most vulnerable, and he will give you a false sense of peace and emotional stability and support during these times. However, he is just waiting on the right opportunity to deceive you and sift you as wheat. Satan usually observes when he thinks he has you emotionally wrapped up in him; then you will begin to see his narcissistic side as he starts to control and manipulate you. Satan wants you to see him as the hero who rescued you when nobody else cared. He uses that vulnerable season and time when he met you to remind you that he was the only one that wants you or cares for you to keep you entrapped in his demonic narcissistic world. You have allowed fear and loneliness to keep you in an abusive relationship where by now you know that God is not present, and God doesn't ordain this relationship. But you just can't seem to get out of this dead, toxic relationship. So you stay in it and continue to be lied to and deceived by Satan and his cohorts of darkness.

How Can Christians Overcome Satan's Attacks While Dating?

Seek God First. Matthew 6:33 reminds us to put God before relationships so He can direct your paths.

Stay in Prayer and in the Word of God. Spiritual discernment protects you against lies and deceit. Pray as well as watch, and be vigilant especially when it seems too good to be true.

Set Boundaries from Day One. Set emotional, physical, and spiritual boundaries to help avoid temptation, and stick to them. Don't allow someone to come into your life and change who God has made you to be in Him since you came to know him. Always remember Psalms 139:14: "I praise you because I am fearfully and wonderfully made; your works are wonderful, I know that full well." Know who you are in Christ. Never lose your identity in Christ. Never forget who you represent here on Earth.

Surround Yourself with Wise Counsel. This mean godly mentors and friends who live what they preach. It means Christians who you share the same faith, who can give you wisdom, knowledge, and understanding to examine your relationship and your relationship goals to see if you are aligning your lifestyle or relationship with the Word of God.

Learn to Wait on the Lord. Rushing into a new relationship after a recent breakup can lead to another heartbreak, so it's worth waiting for God's plans for your life, especially if you are just getting out of a toxic, deceptive relationship or have recently gone through a divorce. Allow yourself a chance to heal from that broken relationship or marriage. Don't carry that same previous baggage into the new relationship.

Fulfillment of God's Plan. When God created Adam and Eve in His image and gave them dominion over the Earth, He intended that they populate and govern the planet. Men cannot produce children with men, and women cannot produce children with women. This is where sexual immorality comes in; if you are in a relationship that cannot reproduce, it's probably not a God-ordained relationship or marriage.

God's Desire Was to Expand His Kingdom on Earth. By multiplying, Adam and Eve would contribute to the growth and expansion of God's creation and His kingdom on Earth. God always had a plan from the beginning before he formed Adam and Eve in the Garden of Eden. Just like when we come up with ideas for our ventures and businesses or have visions for our children and grandchildren's future, God had a plan before the foundation of this world for humanity and how he envisioned us loving him, worshipping him, and fellowshipping with him. The God we serve still desires this relationship with us today.

This is why He created us in His image. His desire for us was to represent Him and look like Him on Earth and have his likeness in the Spirit realm to do good and not evil. His desire for us on Earth was for us to walk like Him, talk like Him, look like Him, and love like Him, and he desired that our minds become like His mind so that we may think like Him. Paul said, *"Let this mind be in you, which was also in Christ Jesus."* (Philippians 2:5)

Jesus also taught his disciples how to pray *"Thy kingdom come. Thy will be done on earth, as it is in heaven."* (Matthew 6:10)

God was in His kingdom in Heaven, but he was lonely, and he approached the heavenly host saying, *"Let us make man in our image, after our likeness. And let them have dominion over the fish of the sea and over the birds of the heavens and over the livestock and over all the earth and over every creeping thing that creeps on the earth."* (Genesis 1:26)

God's Original Plan for Adam and Eve was to cultivate and subdue the Earth. God commanded them to "be fruitful and multiply," which was part of a bigger picture and mandate to "fill the earth with humans and subdue it," meaning that humanity was to cultivate the land and exercise responsible stewardship over the earth (Genesis 1:28).

CONCLUSION

Taking Authority and Recognizing Satan's Tactics Daily

MANY CHRISTIANS DON'T walk or live the fullness of their Christian walk of freedom due to fear and attacks by Satan while facing daily challenges. In the parable of the sower, the Word of God describes how Satan, or the cares of this world, can "choke" or hinder the Word of God from taking root and bearing fruit in the Christian life (Matthew 13:18–23).

Christians must be aware of the spiritual warfare daily. Do not become victim to Satan's well-planned and well-considered traps for your life. Satan knows where your weaknesses are, just like he knew Eve's weakness in the Garden of Eden. He will come to tempt or seduce you with his worldly devices. These unclean spirits are masterful in warfare. This is why we must put on the whole armor of God (Ephesians 6:10–18).

Satan transforms himself into an angel of light such as a priest or apostle to deceive you with his intentions toward you. I can tell you from experience that I have been tempted by Satan through someone wearing a collar on many occasions. Praise God that I am filled with the Holy Spirit and was able to discern their spirit by the spirit of God. I was able recognize that they were trying to come into my life to rob, steal, or kill. We must recognize that Satan has an army that understands our desires and our needs, so he will send someone who might appear to be an answer to your prayers.

As believers, we are not called to live in fear but to walk in the authority God has given us. Jesus declared in Luke 10:19, *"Behold, I give unto you power to tread on serpents and scorpions, and over all the power of the enemy: and nothing shall by any means hurt you."*

This is not a passive suggestion—it is a divine command to stand firm against the enemy.

You must affirm your faith each day by putting on the whole armor of God, ensuring that you are fortified against the schemes of Satan and his cohorts of darkness. Be prayerful, stay vigilant, for, as 1 Peter 5:8 warns, *"Be sober, be vigilant; because your adversary the devil, as a roaring lion, walketh about, seeking whom he may devour."* But do not be intimidated; resist the devil, and he will flee from you (James 4:7). Satan doesn't care that you have a prayer life every day; he will still challenge you, and you still will have to go through trials and tribulations.

The Word of God declares that *"Man that is born of a woman is of few days, and full of trouble. He cometh forth like a flower and is cut down; He fleeth also as a shadow, and continueth not."* (Job 14:1)

"Many are the afflictions of the righteous, but the Lord delivers him out of them all."

—Psalm 34:19

No one is exempt from Satan's attacks. You are not called to live in fear, defeat, or uncertainty. God has already given you the power to overcome Satan—not just occasionally, but every single day. Jesus declared in Luke 10:19, *"Behold, I give you power to tread on serpents and scorpions, and over all the power of the enemy: and nothing shall by any means hurt you."* If you are filled with the Holy Spirit, God has given you the power! Use it to put Satan and his cohorts of darkness under your feet.

This is your divine inheritance. Jesus Christ has already defeated Satan on the cross; when Christ got up with all power in his hands (Colossians 2:15) and now it is your responsibility to enforce your victory. Satan thrives in deception, distractions, and discouragement, but you have the authority and "dominus" power by the Holy Spirit to shut him down before he even begins his attack! Sometimes God will warn you through dreams and visions through the Holy Spirit.

The Word of God says, *"But when he, the Spirit of truth, comes, he will guide you into all the truth."* (John 16:13)

The Holy Spirit helps us to learn and remember the teachings of our Lord and Savior Jesus Christ. In Order to Be Victorious Over Satan, You Must Take Action.

Your Daily Action Plan for Walking in Authority

"Put on the full armor of God that ye may be able to stand against the wiles of the devil."
—Ephesians 6:11

Before you start your day, cover yourself with the belt of truth, breastplate of righteousness, shield of faith, helmet of salvation, and the sword of the Spirit. Without them, you are vulnerable—with them, you are unstoppable. As believers, we are engaged in spiritual warfare every day. Satan knows we belong to God and is constantly seeking ways to attack our minds, health, finances, family, marriages, and any relationship that represents Christ. Satan's desire is to weaken our faith and distract us from our destiny and God's purpose for us. God has given us His divine wisdom and knowledge to stand against Satan's attacks against us.

Speak and declare God's Word over your life and your family's life daily. Jesus defeated Satan in the wilderness by speaking the Word (Matthew 4:4). You must do the same. Every morning, declare God's promises over your life, family, health, and finances. *"No weapon formed against you shall prosper!"* (Isaiah 54:17)

Pray with Authority. The enemy fears a praying believer. Use the authority given to you in Matthew 18:18: *"Whatever you bind on earth shall be bound in heaven, and whatever you loose on earth* *shall be loosed in heaven."* Bind Satan's attacks and loose God's power over your life!

Walk in Holiness and Righteousness. Sin gives Satan access to your life. But when you walk in obedience, he has no legal right to touch you (James 4:7). Submit to God, resist the devil, and he will flee!

Stay spiritually alert. Satan is crafty, but he is also predictable. He uses fear, confusion, temptation, and distractions to pull you away from God. But you will not be ignorant of his devices (2 Corinthians 2:11). Stay vigilant and discern his tactics before they take root!

Take every thought captive. The battlefield is your mind. Do not entertain thoughts of doubt, fear, or defeat. Instead, bring every thought into obedience to Christ (2 Corinthians 10:5). Speak life, speak truth, and cast out every lie of Satan and claim your victory!

Being victorious over Satan and his cohorts of darkness is not a one-time event; it is a lifestyle that we must apply daily. You have been given the divine dominus authority—use it. Walk boldly, live, and walk upright before the Lord, and never allow the enemy to deceive you. You were born to be a conqueror in Christ Jesus. Now, rise up, take your stand, and walk in the dominion that God has given you! *"Greater is he that is in you than he that is in the world."* (1 John 4:4)

P.O. Box 453
Powder Springs, Georgia 30127
www.entegritypublishing.com
info@entegritypublishing.com
404.472.9190

www.ingramcontent.com/pod-product-compliance
Lightning Source LLC
Chambersburg PA
CBHW061127100726
47911CB00013B/714

* 9 7 9 8 9 9 9 1 6 6 8 0 7 *